MYSTERY IN THE SNOW

Dedication

*This book is dedicated to Andrew, Laura
and Matthew, the most important
people in my life.*

Mystery in the Snow

J. M. EVANS

DERNIER PUBLISHING
Tonbridge

Copyright © J.M. Evans 2009

First published 2009

Published by Dernier Publishing
P.O. Box 403, Tonbridge, TN9 9BJ, England
www.dernierpublishing.com

ISBN 978 0 9536963 3 8

Cover illustration by Maureen Carter

Book design and production for the publisher by
Bookprint Creative Services, <www.bookprint.co.uk>
Printed in Great Britain.

Contents

ONE
The Stolen Bike

"Are you going to play football on the computer *all* evening?" complained Debbie. She stared at the back view of her brother Joel and their two friends, Ravi and Lance, and sighed loudly. "Can't we do something else, all together?"

"Like what?" asked Joel without turning round, his dark curly hair bouncing in excitement as he gained possession of the ball and aimed for the net. "*Oh, did you see that goal!*" He cheered loudly and the other boys congratulated him.

"Well, that's it, you've definitely won, Joel," admitted Lance, running his hands through his fair hair. "You're too good for me. Do you want a go, Rav?"

"No, it's OK. Joel would beat me anyway!"

"That's only 'cause he spends half his life playing it," muttered Debbie, but Joel only grinned.

"The best half of my life!" he sighed contentedly, turning off the computer and flopping into a soft armchair. "I'm glad our mums don't mind having their prayer meeting in the dining room, or we wouldn't get the decent chairs and the computer!"

Ravi looked at his watch. "What shall we do now?

We've still got about an hour."

"Can't we just chill?" asked Joel. "This is the first evening of the holidays."

"We'll chill properly if we get the snow they're talking about," said Lance with a grin. "I hope we get loads, we'll need something to do."

"No youth club for three weeks," sighed Ravi. "How boring is that? And I can't even go out on my bike, now it's been stolen!"

Joel stretched himself out lazily. "I can't wait to do nothing," he yawned. "Plus, we get Easter eggs next weekend! All that chocolate! Anyway, if it does snow, we've got to deliver parcels, remember?" Everyone nodded. Tina, the youth club leader, had made an arrangement; if it did snow, as was forecast, the young people would pick up food parcels from the church and take them round to elderly people who couldn't get out.

"I hope the snow will be thick enough to go sledging in the park," said Debbie. "We've got a sledge, I think it's in the loft."

Ravi nodded eagerly. "And we can have snowball fights! Even delivering parcels might be fun in the snow."

"As long as we don't get Mrs Adamson to deliver to," agreed Joel.

"Why?" asked Ravi. "What's the matter with her?"

"She's scary," answered Joel with feeling. "She lives next door to the park and if anyone's ball goes in her garden, she doesn't let them have it back. You know

Vince, from school? He knocked on her door once for a dare, asked for his football back. She waved her walking stick at him, shut the door in his face and the next day his appendix burst!"

"You're not saying she had anything to do with his appendix?" laughed Ravi.

"Well, people said so at the time!"

Ravi looked at him scathingly. "You don't really believe that though?"

"No, I suppose I don't!" admitted Joel, laughing. "But you know, she does glare at you as if she'd like to turn you into a toad!" He did an impression of a fat-faced toad, which made the other boys laugh.

"That is so mean!" protested Debbie. "I know she never smiles, but that doesn't mean she's horrible."

"Well, she's wrinkled and bent over and she's got a big nose," said Joel, grinning rather sheepishly.

"You read too many fairy stories!" said Ravi. "I think we ought to ask if we can deliver to her. After the talk at Club yesterday – you know, Jesus visiting Zacchaeus, us being kind to people nobody likes?"

"No way!" said Joel. "Anyway, we don't get to choose; Tina said she'd text us and give us someone. If we get her, I'm not going. She might wave her walking stick at me and turn me into something nasty!"

"Too late," declared Debbie. "You're already something nasty!" They all fell about laughing as Debbie handed round the biscuit tin.

"Talking of nasty people," said Ravi, "you know that quiz we did at youth club? Who did you all put for the person you would least like to buy a birthday present for?"

"That was easy," said Debbie immediately. "Gerry, in my class. She thinks she's It, she thinks she knows everything and she pushes in the dinner queue. How about you?"

Lance grimaced. "My dad's new partner, Helen. She buys me things my mum can't afford and I have to say thank you or Dad has a go at me for being ungrateful. Mum made me give her a present last Christmas. I'd made up my mind I wouldn't ever do that again, but I suppose I'll have to now." He sighed ruefully.

"I couldn't think of anyone," admitted Joel, "so I put in tax collectors."

"Tax collectors?" laughed Ravi. "There's no such thing any more!"

"There is," argued Joel, "you just don't see them, because they sit in offices!"

"Trust you to come up with something stupid," groaned Debbie. "How about you, Rav?"

"Well, I was going to put the evil people who force children to work in factories," replied Ravi. "But in the end I put the thief who stole my bike and the other things from our shed."

"I can understand that," agreed Debbie and the others nodded too.

"Being kind to people who don't deserve it is really

hard," said Ravi with a frown. "I can understand why nobody would want to go to Zacchaeus' house. Who'd want to visit a liar, thief and cheat?"

"And I should be nice to Helen!" moaned Lance.

"And I've got to forgive the criminal who stole my bike," sighed Ravi. "That's not easy, I can tell you!"

"Maybe we should try and find out who did steal it," suggested Debbie.

"Why?" asked Joel, grinning. "So we can give him a birthday present?"

"No, Stupid," groaned Debbie, pulling a face in her brother's direction. "*To get the bike back!*"

"I'd like to," agreed Ravi, "but it was already two nights ago. The thief will have long gone. There have been other burglaries from sheds round here, though," he mused. "Perhaps we could set up a trap?"

"In *our* shed!" yelled Joel, jumping up.

"You mean now?" asked Debbie. "But it's freezing out there!"

"So what? It's a brilliant idea," said Lance, nearly spilling his drink in his excitement.

"You wanted to do something all together, Debs," Ravi reminded her.

Debbie's eyes shone. "This is just the sort of thing," she agreed. "Solving a mystery!"

"I know what!" exclaimed Joel, dumping his glass on the table with a splash. "I got a room alarm last Christmas in a spy kit, we can use that!"

Ravi grabbed his trainers. "And what if we put mud round the shed door to get footprints? Some might be the same as round my shed! You can come round and we'll check tomorrow, I'm sure you'll be allowed. What do you think?"

"Excellent idea," agreed Lance.

"And I'll get my lip gloss!" yelled Debbie, aiming for the door. The boys made faces at each other.

"Your *what*?" asked Joel.

"Lip gloss – smear it on stuff in our shed, get fingerprints!" explained Debbie.

"Oh, right!" laughed Ravi.

"Good idea, Sis," admitted Joel, grabbing a handful of biscuits from the tin. "I'll get the torches and room alarm, back in a minute!" But Lance stopped him.

"We should pray about it first. We know God answers prayer – we've proved that, although we knew it anyway," he added.

The others nodded in excitement. "Well let's pray then," said Debbie, as they all sat back down. "Then we'll get on with the job."

"OK!" said Ravi. "Dear Lord, we know stealing's not right and we pray that I'll be able to get my bike back."

"And please keep us safe from danger," added Debbie.

"Amen," agreed everyone.

"This is going to be such fun!" said Joel, leaping up again. "I can't wait to go to Ravi's tomorrow and look at the crime scene!"

Ravi laughed. "What happened to you wanting to do nothing?"

"This is different!" replied Joel, running upstairs. "This is a real mystery to solve. Oh, I've got another idea – we could put banana skins on the path for burglars to slip on! Help yourselves from the fruit bowl, everyone, back in a minute!"

TWO

The Scene of the Crime

"You're here at last!" said Ravi, greeting his three friends the following afternoon. "Come in and tell me about the trap; catch anybody last night? I haven't visited the crime scene – I thought we should go out all together."

"We didn't exactly catch a burglar . . ." replied Debbie cautiously, bending down to pat Ravi's little black dog, Willow, who was greeting the friends enthusiastically with jumps and licks.

"What do you mean by that?" asked Ravi. Suddenly he stopped, noticing that Joel looked paler and less cheerful than usual and his jacket was hanging at an odd angle. "Are you OK, Joel?"

"He slipped on his own banana skin," giggled Debbie as she took off her coat. Lance couldn't help smiling and Ravi let out a roar of laughter, but Joel grimaced, cradling his left arm, which was in a sling under his jacket.

"Does it hurt?" asked Ravi, realising that actually, if Joel was in pain, it might not be all that funny.

"It's killing me," groaned Joel. "And I'm tired, I need to sit down."

"Oh, sorry for laughing," said Ravi. "Come into the conservatory and tell me everything. We're allowed to have it as our office for as long as we want."

"I think it's called an Operations Room if it's for crime solving," Lance corrected him.

"OK, Operations Room then. So tell me about the banana skin!"

"I can't believe I did it," said Joel, with a yawn, sitting himself down gingerly into a padded wicker chair. "Half the night waiting to see the doctor in the hospital, which was boring, boring, so boring there isn't a word for it and all the time I was in agony! I can't ride a bike for six whole weeks – no running, no football – even football on the computer's going to be difficult, 'cause you need two hands."

"You're joking, that's awful," said Ravi.

"Is it really broken? You haven't got it in plaster!" remarked Lance.

"It's the elbow, it's cracked; you can see the crack on the x-ray, but because of where it is they can't plaster it," sighed Joel, looking round at the others gloomily. "And, while we're talking about it, you've got to be careful," he warned. "If my arm gets knocked it *really* hurts. And I mean *badly*!"

"So nobody else went in your shed then?" asked Ravi.

"Only Dad!" admitted Debbie.

"Oh no!" exclaimed Ravi. "I hope you told him about the trap?"

Joel grimaced. "We didn't get a chance, 'cause he was working late. How could we have known that he'd go and get logs for the fire? He does that, like, once in a million years."

"We were well in trouble," Debbie admitted. "When the alarm went off it made Dad jump and he hit his head on the shed roof. He was well cross."

"And he got lip gloss on his jacket and mud on his work shoes," added Joel, managing a small smile. "We didn't tell him you put extra mud round, Rav!"

Ravi grinned back. "What about the banana skin then?"

Joel yawned widely. "I had to turn off the alarm and I forgot it was there. We're going to have to watch it for few days – if anything else bad happens, me and Debs will get grounded."

"Looking round Rav's garden can't hurt anybody," reasoned Lance. "Everybody ready now?"

"I hope this bit of crime-solving is more successful than our first effort!" said Joel, struggling to get out of his chair.

"It will be," Ravi assured him. "As it's muddy round the shed, there may be footprints. Maybe we can do rubbings or sketches."

Debbie gave a yell. "No need for that, I can use the camera on my new phone!"

"This sounds exciting," said Ravi's mum, Harita, popping her head round the door. "Hello everyone! Nice to see you all, but no getting into trouble, OK? Your mum's just phoned me, Joel – I'm sorry about your elbow."

"Thank you," replied Joel, rather pathetically. They all grinned when Harita left, even Joel. This wasn't going to be trouble, this was going to be fun! And how brilliant it would be if they could get Ravi's bike back!

"What else was stolen, apart from your bike?" asked Lance as Ravi slid open the patio doors.

"My sister's trike, the lawnmower, some other garden tools and all our garden chairs."

"Wow, did they leave anything?" asked Debbie.

"Not much!" said Ravi with a grin, leading the way to the shed. "A few plant pots, spiders, that sort of thing! Poor Gita, she's really upset about her trike."

Apart from a small patio next to the house, most of Ravi's garden was laid to lawn. Rectangular in shape, it was the width of the house and about three times as long, with flower beds edging the grass on each side. A straight path made its way from the house to the top of the garden where the shed stood and a gate opened on to a passageway which ran along the backs of the gardens to the road. Muddy patches had been worn into the grass around the shed and the gate, which were now fastened with bright new padlocks. The little group stopped a metre or so away and surveyed the scene. "Footprints!" yelled Lance suddenly, bending down to the ground and pointing towards the muddy patches. "Stay here, Willow, no walking on the evidence!"

"Look!" said Debbie excitedly. "The footprints are different patterns; this one's got circles, these ones are ridges . . . "

"And over here, if you look carefully, you can see zigzags!" yelled Lance, moving towards the shed. "See there? That makes three different prints!"

"That'll be mine, Dad's . . . and the burglar's!" yelled Ravi excitedly.

"Didn't the police look round?" asked Lance.

"No, they just made a list of what was missing."

"So it's not their footprints then?" Ravi shook his head as Debbie edged closer to take some photos.

"These are mine," said Ravi, pointing out the ridged set of footprints after checking the bottom of his trainers. Suddenly Joel gave a yell.

"There are some really obvious ones over here, by the gate, with zigzags!"

"Those shoes are way too big for mine and Dad's," decided Ravi, inspecting the footprints carefully.

"So they have to be the criminal's!" crowed Debbie delightedly. "Do you think he was working alone?"

"Looks like it," nodded Lance, "unless other people were in a van, waiting to take away the stuff."

"I can't believe we've actually got some evidence!" said Joel. "Shall we check outside the gate too?" Nodding, Ravi unlocked the padlocked gate and they all filed through into the passageway. Taking care not to mess up any clues, they made their way along the edges of the path towards the road. There were plenty of footprints in the mud of all sizes and shapes; it was difficult to distinguish one set from another, but sure enough there were more of the footprints with the zigzag pattern. And there was another discovery which made Ravi gasp.

"My bike!" he yelled, pointing out the print of bicycle tyres disappearing off towards the road, partially obliterated now. He looked round at his friends and said again rather sadly, "That was probably my bike!" The others nodded sympathetically and Debbie took some more pictures, then compared them with the ones she had taken by the shed.

"The zigzag footprints here are definitely the same as the ones in the garden," she confirmed, passing her phone round.

"Wow, they really are!" said Ravi, shaking his head. "I can't believe I wasted so much time before checking this out!"

"How awful to just help yourself to other people's bikes," observed Lance.

"We're going to get mine back though!" said Ravi, with feeling.

"At least we're on the right path," said Joel, then realising what he had said, he grinned and pointed at the ground. "Get it, on the right path?" The others groaned.

"Good to see you back to normal, Joel," grinned Lance. He went to give Joel's arm a friendly punch, but Joel recoiled in horror.

"*Mind my arm!*" he yelled, then heaved a sigh of relief as Lance remembered, just in time. "Wow, that was close!

You keep away from me! If that means no more jokes, fine!"

Debbie grinned. "No more jokes, that sounds good!"

"Come on everyone, stay focused," urged Ravi, leading the way back to his garden. "Shed next!"

As Ravi had said earlier, the shed was almost empty now. It was cold, dark and quiet inside, with cobwebs in the corners and pale green ivy pushing its way through a crack near the window. Willow sniffed round too. At first there didn't seem to be anything interesting to see at all, but then suddenly Debbie saw it, in a crack of wood above the door.

"I've found something!" she screeched, reaching up. "Look at this!"

THREE
Following the Plan

As everyone crowded round, Debbie carefully removed a lock of light-coloured hair from a jagged piece of wood above the shed door. "Look at that!" she crowed, holding up the few strands of hair. "It's curly, too!"

"That is not mine!" laughed Ravi. "Or Dad's!" Everyone grinned. The thought of any of Ravi's family with curly fair hair was quite ridiculous!

"The burglar must have got his hair caught in the wood," said Lance. "Ouch, that must have hurt!"

"Serves him right," announced Ravi cheerfully. "He shouldn't have been in here." After another search of the garden that revealed nothing more of interest, they went back to the conservatory. "Two excellent clues," said Ravi, "that's fantastic! Give me your jackets, I'll put them in the hall. Make yourselves comfortable and we'll decide what to do next."

"As the hair's not grey, the burglar must be young," Joel commented, easing himself carefully once more into one of the padded chairs.

"Not necessarily," countered Lance. "My mum's nearly forty and she hasn't got any grey hair."

"Dyes it, probably," said Debbie. Lance looked

23

astonished.

"Really?"

"Let's just say under forty then," said Joel quickly, before anyone could start a discussion about hair dye. "So we're looking for a young to middle-aged man with big feet and curly fair hair. Know anyone like that?" Everybody racked their brains, but shook their heads.

"So now what do we do?" asked Ravi.

"I made a list of ideas last night," Lance replied, producing a rather crumpled sheet of paper from his pocket. "Shall I read it? Although I have to say, I think we're being a bit optimistic. I mean, it'll be good fun and everything, but actually finding the things and getting them back . . ."

"Hey, where's your faith?" asked Debbie. "We prayed about it, remember?"

"I don't think faith means you get everything you ask for," countered Lance.

"Oh let's not talk too much," said Joel, "We certainly won't get the bike back unless we get on with some action."

"I agree," said Ravi. "It would be good to get Gita's trike back too, if we can. What's on your list then, Lance?"

Lance carefully unfolded his sheet of paper. "We've done number one, look round Ravi's garden. Number two, look on the Internet, see if we can find Ravi's bike for sale. Gita's trike too, I guess."

Ravi whistled. "That's clever. We can do that now!"

Lance grinned at him.

"I'm not finished yet! Three. Check the second-hand bike shop in town – the one behind the new coffee shop – see if the bike's ended up there." Everyone nodded enthusiastically. "Four. See if we can find out about other people whose sheds were broken into, see if there are any distinguishing marks . . ."

"What do you mean, distinguishing marks?" interrupted Debbie.

"Like, were padlocks cut off in the same way, things like that. Then we'd know if it was the same thief."

"Oh right," said Debbie. "That's impressive."

"Brilliant!" agreed Joel. "I couldn't have put it better myself. So shall we start by looking on the Internet?"

"There's one last thing," said Lance. "Number five. We need to get into the mind of the criminal." There was a puzzled silence.

"Do what?" asked Joel.

"We need to think, if you were them, what would you take and why? That sort of thing."

"I don't want to sound thick," said Debbie, "but how's that going to help us?"

"I'm not sure yet," admitted Lance, "but we need to think about it. Knowing the motive might be useful."

"I think we need to stop thinking and get on with it!" said Joel impatiently, jumping up, then groaning in pain. Willow, who had been sitting at Joel's feet, jumped up too and wagged her tail.

"Willow wants action!" said Debbie. "So can we use the computer, Rav?"

"I'll ask Mum to do the password," nodded Ravi. "And I'll check Dad's trainers for the tread – make sure the other footprints are his and not a second burglar."

"Good idea," agreed Lance. "How about you and Debbie check the shoes, me and Joel check the Internet?"

"Then we can all go to the bike shop together," nodded Ravi. "Willow can come with us – walkies is just the sort of action she likes!"

*   *   *

Later that evening, alone in his little bedroom, Lance sighed with satisfaction. It had been a great day – finding the footprints and the strands of hair had been amazing! The Internet search for Ravi's bike had been fun, so had looking through the local newspaper for information and the man at the bike shop had been really helpful. They still had just the two clues – the footprints and the hair, but it was a great start! They had had a fantastic dinner too – Harita made the best curries ever. Lance grinned to himself as he remembered Joel spilling rice everywhere, making everyone laugh because he could only use one arm.

Now, as they had all promised each other, Lance set his mind to thinking about what they could do next to catch the bike thief. But as he lay on his bed and pondered the problem, he began to feel uncomfortable. If this man was a criminal, he could be dangerous. Looking for criminals wasn't a game. The others had seemed so sure that once they had prayed about it, everything would be fine. But could they just assume that everything would be OK if they prayed about it?

With an uncomfortable feeling in his stomach, Lance prayed, "If we shouldn't be trying to get Ravi's bike back, Lord, please show us. It's been fun," he added, sadly, "but it would be awful if something bad happened. Please show us what to do, if what we're doing is wrong. Amen."

He felt a bit better after praying. He knew God understood. With a sigh, Lance got up to close his curtains, then stopped in surprise as he noticed a handful of snowflakes drift past his bedroom window. "Mum, it's snowing!" he yelled. Anna came in from the kitchen, still wearing her yellow rubber gloves.

"It is!" she smiled. They stood for a while, leaning on the window sill together in companionable silence. The snowflakes weren't light and floaty for long; soon they were falling thick and fast and a layer of snow began to settle on the roofs of the flats opposite and on the cars parked two floors down on the street below.

"Looks like you'll be delivering those parcels to the old people tomorrow," said Anna. Yes, thought Lance, they would. Well, that would keep them from the bike problem for a while. Maybe the snow was the answer to his prayer.

FOUR

Snow!

"I thought we were supposed to be getting global warming," Debbie complained next morning as she, Joel, Ravi and Lance left the church building, carrying several supermarket bags between them. "It's freezing out here!"

"Walk in the sun, not the shade," suggested Ravi. "It's warmer."

"It's all right for you," grumbled Joel, struggling to keep up with the others through the ankle deep snow. "You've no idea how hard it is walking with only one arm. I wish I could cycle!"

"Surely as long as you've got two legs you're OK?" reasoned Lance. "You don't walk on your arms!"

"Yeah, well, you balance with your arms," replied Joel, a little grumpily. "And it's just our luck to get Mrs Adamson to deliver to," he added. "I thought Tina liked us!"

"Oh stop going on about Mrs Adamson," snapped Debbie. "I thought you weren't going to come if we got her, so why don't you just go back home and be selfish and play computer games? We're carrying all the bags without you anyway!"

"Good idea, Debs, you've persuaded me," said Joel,

turning back immediately.

"Oh come with us, Joel," urged Lance, "it won't be the same without you! We don't mind carrying the bags, do we, Rav?"

"'Course not!" replied Ravi. "It's not far."

"Well, all right. But I'll stand at the back, so if she starts anything funny with her stick, she'll miss me and get you lot!"

"Look, this ought to be fun," reasoned Ravi, "so let's look on the bright side. I can't cycle either 'cause my bike's been stolen, but it is the holidays and we have got snow!"

"I agree. Let's get the parcel bit over with quickly," said Lance. "We've only got to drop off the food, then we can go and have fun in the park! We'll go in the side entrance, it's just round the corner from Mrs Adamson's."

"Then we can discuss how we're going to get my bike back," said Ravi. Debbie and Joel nodded, but Lance kept quiet.

"Let's see what's in the parcel," he suggested, wanting to change the subject.

"It's hardly a parcel – collection of bags more like," commented Debbie, stopping to open the one she was carrying. "I've got butter, strawberry jam, a tin of chicken soup and some bread. It's a real fresh loaf – smells delicious, mmm, I could eat a slice of that right now!"

Ravi peered into his bags. "I've got cheese, tea bags, sugar, milk, and in this one . . . a tin of rice pudding, some black grapes, a packet of chocolate biscuits and a bag of marshmallows! Wow, that's nice!"

Lance rifled through his bags. "I've got potatoes, tomatoes, a carton of orange juice, a box of apple pies and . . . ooh, eggs, bacon and sausages! Do you think that's a good idea for old people? All that fat clogging up their arteries?"

"Our grandad has bacon and eggs for breakfast every morning!" laughed Debbie. "He won't eat cereal, calls it rabbit food!"

"Hey, we could have fun with this lot," said Joel, with a gleam in his eyes. "How about we skip Mrs Adamson's, go up to the woods and have a camp fire?"

"Don't be silly, the church isn't giving out parcels for us!" scoffed Lance.

"And get real, we wouldn't be allowed a camp fire," agreed Debbie gloomily. "Pity, 'cause I love toasting marshmallows. Don't you just love them when they're all crisp on the outside and gooey in the middle?" Then suddenly she brightened. "But we might be allowed to have a bonfire in our garden later!"

"That would be fun, in the snow!" said Ravi. "Ask your parents, yeah? Hey, isn't this Mrs Adamson's road?" It was. As they turned into Salisbury Mews, everything suddenly became quieter. Apart from one man in a navy blue suit going from door to door, the road was empty. The noise of traffic swishing through the slush on the main road grew dimmer and the crunch of snow under their boots now echoed off the neat red-brick houses on both sides of the road. Sparrows pecked at bread left out in a front garden and fluttered about squabbling, but apart from the birds, everything was almost eerily still. "Mrs Adamson's is right at the end, number one," said Ravi, breaking the silence.

"Next to the park," said Joel, looking at Lance. "How's your appendix?"

Lance grinned back. "You going to knock on the door then, Joel?" he asked.

"Me? No way! You can!"

"She does know we're coming?" checked Ravi, hesitating at the gate to number one.

Lance nodded. "Tina phoned."

"Oh for goodness sake, I'll knock," said Debbie impatiently, pushing the others out of the way and striding up the short path. "Honestly, you boys are such wimps!" The door bell sounded loud in the stillness and the four stared anxiously at the wooden door for what seemed like ages.

"Shame, she's not at home, we'll have to eat the food ourselves," said Joel, turning away, but Debbie motioned with her arm.

"I can hear something," she hissed. Slowly the door opened. There was a moment's silence while Mrs Adamson glared suspiciously at the little group through her gold-rimmed glasses. She was wearing a black woolly dress and cardigan and was leaning on her walking stick.

"Watch the stick!" muttered Joel under his breath. Lance suppressed a laugh.

"What are you sniggering at?" asked Mrs Adamson rather harshly. "Are you the children from church with the shopping?"

"That's us!" replied Debbie breezily, giving a bright smile. "Except we're not really children, we're young people." There was another moment's silence, while Mrs Adamson lowered her eyebrows and glowered at Debbie and the boys with her dark beady eyes.

"You look like children to me!" she retorted. They all took a step backwards as the old lady leaned forward and began to lift her stick slightly. For a fleeting moment, Lance saw what Joel meant about Mrs Adamson; she was looking at them as if she'd like to turn them into toads!

Debbie swallowed and said quickly, "Shall we bring the bags in or do you want to take them?" Mrs Adamson relaxed a little.

"You can come in," she said stiffly. "The kitchen's straight ahead." She turned and led the way down the hall. The friends looked round at each other in alarm.

"We haven't got to go in, have we?" asked Ravi.

"Hurry up," called Mrs Adamson sharply. "Close the front door, it's cold out there, in case you hadn't noticed!"

"You've done it this time, Debs," hissed Joel, as Debbie shrugged her shoulders and led the way into the house.

The kitchen was warm and looked clean and neat, but there was an overpowering smell of cooking fish, which almost made it difficult to breathe. A wooden clock ticked loudly on a shelf and a sudden hiss of steam escaping from a saucepan on the cooker made Lance jump. The boys made faces at each other. Debbie glared at them, then she noticed a plump tortoiseshell cat with long white whiskers and a feathery tail, sitting on a patchwork cushion on an old-fashioned wooden chair. Seeing the visitors, the cat stood up, yawned, stretched in an elegant fashion and mewed a greeting.

"Oh, what a beautiful cat!" crooned Debbie, dumping her shopping on the table and going over to stroke the cat, who began to purr loudly. "I wish we could have a cat. We can't though, 'cause Mum's allergic to their fur."

"I'd love one, but I've already got a dog!" said Ravi with a sigh. "I'm not allowed to have a cat as well."

Lance nodded sympathetically. "We're not allowed any pets in our flat, but I've always wanted a cat. This one's really cute! What's her name?"

"Lucy," Mrs Adamson informed them, sounding pleased. "She was a stray. I've had her nearly a year now."

"That's nice," said Ravi politely as he and Joel joined the others. "She's quite chubby, isn't she?"

"When she first came she was as thin as a rake," retorted Mrs Adamson sharply. "I believe God sent her to me so I could look after her. And she keeps me company." Nobody could think of a reply to that, so they just carried on stroking the cat.

"Well, we'd better go," said Ravi, as soon as it seemed

reasonable. "I hope you enjoy the parcel."

Mrs Adamson nodded. "Would you like a cup of tea?" she asked suddenly. Even Debbie hesitated.

"I think we should be getting back," muttered Joel eventually, avoiding Mrs Adamson's piercing gaze.

"Eh, what's that, young man?" asked Mrs Adamson sharply. "It's no good whispering, nobody will hear you!"

"He said thanks," said Debbie sweetly, "we'd love a cup of tea."

FIVE

A Nasty Shock

The kettle seemed to take forever to boil. The boys sighed, shuffled from foot to foot and made bored faces at each other.

"Well, sit down," Mrs Adamson instructed them all brusquely, as she eventually filled the teapot with water from the kettle. "You're making the place look untidy." The friends reluctantly undid their coats and took seats around the kitchen table. Apart from the squeaking of the chair legs on the shiny floor and the ticking of the clock, the silence was almost deafening. Debbie tried to think of something to say.

"We don't use a teapot at home," she managed eventually. Mrs Adamson gave a disapproving tut, but didn't reply. Joel glared at Debbie as Mrs Adamson joined them at the table and in silence poured milk, then tea, into matching floral cups.

Debbie tried again. "Have you lived here long?"

"Forty years," she replied. "Same as I've been going to the church, where they don't sing enough hymns these days."

"I like the shorter songs," said Lance boldly. "I don't always understand the words of the hymns. One we sang on Sunday said 'ineffably sublime' – I mean, what's that?" For the first time, Mrs Adamson gave a hint of a smile.

"Sometimes the language is old-fashioned, I suppose," she admitted.

Joel said, "You know the hymn 'Amazing Grace'? I used to think it went, 'saved a watch like me'." Mrs Adamson's smile grew broader. Encouraged, Joel continued. "You know it says, 'I once was lost, but now I'm found'? I used to imagine God going round looking for lost watches!" At that point, Mrs Adamson actually gave a little chortle. It was so sudden that Debbie, who was sitting next to her, nearly spilled her tea.

The four drank as quickly as they could, then after a few more stilted remarks about the weather and school, got up to go. They gave Lucy a goodbye stroke, said goodbye to Mrs Adamson at the door, then got outside as quickly as they could. It was lovely to breathe the fresh air again, however cold it felt after the warm kitchen.

"What a stink of fish!" groaned Ravi, as soon as Mrs Adamson had closed the door.

"Did you see Lance jump when the saucepan lid rattled?" laughed Joel. "Maybe something in there was trying to get out!"

"It must be fish for Lucy," grinned Lance, zipping up his jacket. "It didn't smell edible!"

"I thought I was going to throw up," groaned Debbie.

"Serves you right!" said all the boys, more or less in unison.

"How could you have said yes to a cup of tea?" Joel berated her, as they made their way to the park entrance. "I will remember that smell for the rest of my life!"

"Don't be so mean, she seemed lonely," Debbie retorted.

"At least she didn't invite us to dinner!" said Lance and they all creased up laughing and groaning at the thought of eating the contents of the saucepan.

"She had tears in her eyes when we left," said Ravi when they had all regained their composure. "Did you see?"

"No, did she?" asked Lance, surprised. "Why?"

"I think she was sorry we were going," said Debbie. "Maybe she's our tax collector."

"Our *what*?" asked Joel, as they entered the park.

"Our person to visit that nobody else wants to," explained Debbie.

Joel made a face. "Visiting old people's not my thing."

"Nor mine," agreed Ravi.

"Me neither," said Lance.

"Fine," said Debbie huffily, "let's just leave her to be lonely then!"

"Maybe she was crying with relief that we were leaving!" suggested Joel with a grin.

"I think it went well," said Lance, putting on his gloves and making a huge snowball. "We took the food and hopefully cheered her up. But I'm glad it's over." He lobbed the snowball at Joel, who happened not to be looking.

"Hey!" yelled Joel. "Who threw that?" He looked round, but everyone was looking equally innocent. "Right, if none of you owns up, you all get it!" Joel grinned wickedly and even with one arm, managed to get in several good shots before anyone got him back.

It was beautiful in the park. The sun sparkling on the dazzling white snow transformed even the litter bins into something almost fairytale. The trees shimmered in their new finery and the view of the woods and fields beyond the park looked like a scene from a Christmas card. In the park, groups of brightly dressed people were playing on the swings, feeding the ducks by the lake, making snowmen, sledging down the castle mound and chasing each other in the snow, shrieking with laughter. There was a truly festive feel in the air and in the sun it was almost warm.

"I wish we had our sledge," sighed Debbie. "Dad's going to get it out of the loft tonight, so we can have it tomorrow." Ravi nodded enthusiastically.

"That will be good. I've got an idea for today, though – let's build walls in teams, then knock them down with snowballs!"

"I like that idea," nodded Lance. "Best wall wins! Me and Joel against you and Debbie, OK?"

"But that's not fair!" protested Joel. "I've only got one arm!"

"Come on, Joel, we can beat them," encouraged Lance.

"How long do we get to build?"

"Ten minutes, starting . . . NOW!" yelled Ravi. The next few minutes passed quickly as both teams worked furiously. Debbie and Ravi built their wall long and straight; Lance and Joel constructed a series of mounds in a circle, like a ring of headless snowmen. Despite Joel's disability they made a good team – Lance collected the snow into heaps and Joel used his feet to shape and compact the mounds. In consequence, when it came to demolition time, their wall was easily the strongest. Just as Ravi and Debbie were admitting defeat, Ravi's phone rang.

"Hi Tina," Ravi greeted her cheerfully, "we've delivered the parcel!" The others gathered round and watched in consternation as Ravi's expression changed. "OK, we'll be back as soon as we can," he said quietly, then closed his phone. "Mrs Adamson's phoned Tina and wasn't very happy about something," he explained. "Tina's at my house. She's asked if we can go and meet her there."

"Now? Do our parents know?" asked Lance. Ravi nodded and Debbie frowned.

"I don't understand. What could we possibly have done that she didn't like?"

Leaving their snow defences completely forgotten, the little group made their way soberly to Ravi's house, where Harita welcomed them in and took their jackets. Tina, a tall, dark girl in her early twenties, was playing a game of tug-of-war on the conservatory floor with Willow and her green stripy rope. She smiled warmly in greeting at the puzzled group.

"I'm really sorry to bring you back from your fun," she apologised, letting Willow have her toy. "Do you all want to sit down? Something rather upsetting has happened. Mrs Adamson's handbag has gone missing and I'm afraid she thinks one of you took it." The four friends looked at each other in amazement.

"She thinks we stole her handbag?" asked Ravi, thinking he must have heard wrongly.

"I'm afraid so," said Tina, her usually cheerful face creasing into a frown.

"The woman's crazy!" observed Joel. "Quite out of her mind!"

"We didn't have anything to do with any handbag, honest we didn't, Tina," cried Debbie. "You know we wouldn't!"

"Yes, I know," sighed Tina. "I tried to tell Mrs Adamson that, but apparently nobody else went in the house and you passed it on a little table on the way to the kitchen. I don't suppose you saw it? It's made of black leather with a gold clasp." Tina looked round hopefully, but everyone shook their heads.

"Try and remember," said Harita, joining the shocked group.

"I don't even remember a table in the hall," admitted Lance.

"I do," said Debbie. "It had a mirror over it, but I didn't

notice what was on it." Ravi and Joel shrugged and shook their heads.

"Well it's a horrible business," said Tina, "and I'm sorry you had to be involved. Apparently there wasn't anything of value in the bag, so Mrs Adamson's agreed not to contact the police, in case it turns up. She's probably just forgotten that she moved it."

"Old people can be forgetful," agreed Harita. Tina nodded.

"Well I promised Mrs Adamson I'd see you about it, so here I am. Believe me, I'm hating this as much as you are. If it's still snowy on Thursday, do you want to deliver to someone else?"

"I'm not sure I want to deliver to anyone now," said Ravi stubbornly. "I mean, if we're going to get accused of being thieves, what's the point?" There was a short silence. Debbie jutted out her chin defiantly, Lance and Ravi looked sullen and Tina sighed again. Joel broke the silence.

"Why should we care what other people think? We know we're not thieves."

"Well said, Joel," said Tina with a nod. "Why don't you talk about it together and let me know tomorrow, OK? Keep in touch!"

Ravi's mum let Tina out. They heard Harita say in the hall, "Really, Tina, what a shame this had to happen."

"Tina didn't believe we had anything to do with it," said Lance. "You could tell."

"It's all that horrible Mrs Adamson's fault," muttered Debbie mutinously. "I don't know why we ever bothered to try to be nice to her, just to get it thrown back in our faces!"

SIX

Another Accusation

"More news from Tina!" announced Ravi, stamping the snow off his boots at the front door to Lance's flat, the following morning.

"Good news?" asked Lance eagerly. "I've set the chess board up. I thought we could play while we wait for Debbie and Joel – they've got to do chores before they're allowed out. Has the handbag been found?"

"Sadly not," said Ravi, closing the front door. "And Lucy's gone missing – you know, Mrs Adamson's cat?"

"No!"

"Apparently she didn't go home last night," explained Ravi, going through to the living room. "Mrs Adamson's in a right state, apparently."

Lance joined Ravi at the coffee table, where the chess board stood ready. "She doesn't think we took Lucy too?" he asked, with a grin.

"Yup!" said Ravi. "How did you guess? She does!" Lance's face fell.

"No! Really? But that's ridiculous! She watched us leave! We weren't even carrying a bag – does she think we hid her under our coats or something?"

"I give up," said Ravi, shrugging. "Poor cat, though,

stolen and taken away. I'd be upset if that was my Willow."

"I don't suppose she was stolen," said Lance in disbelief. "Friendly cat, but she didn't look like she was worth a lot of money. She probably just wandered off."

"Or got out quick while the going was good," grinned Ravi, then checked himself. "Sorry, that wasn't very nice!"

Lance was too deep in thought to notice. Suddenly he stood up, almost knocking over the chess board and yelled, "Maybe Lucy's injured!"

Ravi made a face. "I hadn't thought of that," he admitted. "Maybe we should go and look for her, just in case."

"Yes, we could do that. Or maybe she's got shut in somewhere, like in a neighbour's shed! We're going to the park anyway after lunch, so we can look over the fence to Mrs Adamson's garden, see if we can see her . . ."

"Track her paw prints!"

"Brilliant idea! Oh, post," added Lance, hearing the mail plop through the letterbox on to the doormat.

"That's it, the postman!" yelled Ravi. Lance frowned.

"That's what?"

"Mrs Adamson knows the handbag burglar, probably, but doesn't suspect him – it could be her postman!" Lance nodded, his eyes shining.

"I bet you're right – oh, hey, I've just thought of something else – do you remember yesterday, in Mrs Adamson's road, there was a man visiting the houses?

Looked like a door-to-door salesman or something. Maybe *he* took the handbag!"

Ravi's eyes opened wide. "I remember him! If we found Lucy and took her back to Mrs Adamson, we could ask her who else went into her house yesterday. She might have had someone delivering something, or maybe a neighbour popped in . . ."

"She might have a cleaning lady . . ."

"Could be anyone. I suppose we'll have to put off looking for my bike," added Ravi rather sadly.

Lance took a deep breath. "Rav, this is really difficult to say, but after investigating about your bike, I got back home and thought about it. It was such a fun day, but I'm not sure we should be looking for criminals – it could be dangerous."

"Oh," said Ravi, taken aback. "I hadn't thought of it like that. I was thinking more about getting the bike back than finding the people who took it."

"But they could be both together."

Ravi thought for a minute. "Yes, I suppose they could," he reflected. "That might not be all that good. But we did pray about it, so surely everything will be OK?"

"I suppose so. But it just doesn't feel right, I don't understand why not."

"Oh."

"Sorry," said Lance.

"That's OK. So you don't think we should look for my bike then?"

"I'm not sure," replied Lance, trying to find the right words to express how he felt. "It's more like, if the Lord was speaking to us about it, if it felt right after praying and we'd read something encouraging from the Bible, it would be different. It's strange, but looking for Lucy feels completely different. That feels definitely right."

Ravi looked wistful. "But I really want my bike back!"

"I know. I would if it was mine. Maybe the police will find it," replied Lance, trying to be encouraging.

"Maybe. Dad's registered it on a website for stolen bikes too, so you never know." Lance nodded.

"Chess then, till the others come?"

* * *

Joel and Debbie arrived an hour or so later with a blue plastic sledge and cheerful greetings, stamping their feet and blowing their noses, affected by the cold air. Ravi and Lance informed the newcomers of the latest news; of Lucy's disappearance, that they had been blamed, but they suspected the man they had seen in Salisbury Mews or someone else who had visited Mrs Adamson's.

"Good one!" said Joel, thinking it was a joke.

"Very funny, ha ha," agreed Debbie, looking for a space to hang up her coat, then stopped as she noticed Lance and Ravi's expressions. She looked at them incredulously. "You mean Lucy's really missing? And Mrs Adamson really thinks we stole her?"

"Honest truth," nodded Ravi.

"What a cheek!" exploded Debbie and Joel shook his head.

"Didn't I warn you about her?"

"Me and Lance think we should look for Lucy though," said Ravi, "in case she's injured or got shut in somewhere. Do you agree?"

"Definitely!" said Debbie immediately. "We can do that! Poor cat. It's not her fault she's got a horrible owner!"

"And we must pray about it before we go," nodded Lance. "We don't know where Lucy is, but God does, so we need to pray that he'll guide us to the right place."

"Let's do that now," suggested Ravi. They clustered round the coffee table. After a short pause, Lance began to pray.

"Dear Lord, please lead us to Lucy so we can take her back home. We know you care about all the animals that you made and we really need your help. Amen."

"Amen," the others agreed.

"And please keep Lucy safe in the meantime," said Debbie.

"And it would be really good if the real handbag thieves were caught," prayed Joel, "so we don't get into any more trouble."

"Yes, Lord, you know we didn't take the handbag or Lucy," said Ravi. "Please make it so she'll know it wasn't us. Amen." Opening his eyes, Ravi added, "I've just remembered something. In my Bible notes this morning, it was about being bold and courageous, like God said to Joshua before the battle of Jericho. Maybe that's what we've got to be now!"

"You can be bold and courageous if you want," said Joel, grimacing. "I'm not – I might break my other elbow!"

"I can't see how we'll have to be bold and courageous looking for a cat," teased Debbie.

"Maybe she's got sharp claws!" laughed Lance as he texted his mum at work, to let her know where they were going.

After an early lunch of cheese sandwiches, large slabs of delicious home-made chocolate cake and a juicy apple each, which had been left out for them, the four left Lance's flat, taking it in turns to pull the sledge along the pavement. It was colder outside than the day before and somehow less cheerful. Most of the snow on the pavements had turned to slush, the sun had disappeared behind a blanket of grey cloud and a biting wind whipped around, finding every chink of bare skin.

"I'm glad I didn't bring Willow," said Ravi, pulling up the collar of his jacket. "She hates the snow." Debbie looked up at the clouds.

"We must find Lucy quickly in case it snows again, or her paw prints will be covered up."

"I think we will," said Lance confidently. "Somehow I really feel the Lord is going to help us!"

The park was quieter than the day before. The holiday

atmosphere had gone and now only a few hardy people were braving the cold, swathed in layers of coats, hats and scarves.

Debbie looked worried. "Do you think Lucy could have survived a night out in this?" she asked as they trudged towards the fence between the park and Mrs Adamson's back garden.

"Probably. Cats find warm places to shelter," said Joel. "If not, well, everyone has to die some time."

"Thanks for that!" snapped Debbie.

"You're welcome," replied Joel politely. "I wouldn't like to find her dead body though. Imagine taking *that* to Mrs Adamson – she'd probably accuse us of killing her!"

"Joel!" the others protested.

"What I like about you is that you're so cheerful!" said Lance with a grin, as they reached the boundary. "Oh, the fence is too high to see over, what are we going to do?"

"It's OK, there are cracks we can look through," Debbie noticed.

"There's a gap here," commented Ravi, peering through the space between a post and a fence panel. "Anybody see anything? All I can see are snow-covered bushes."

Lance, peering through a small hole he had found, suddenly gave a yell. "Yes! Over here, come and look!"

SEVEN

Where Is Lucy?

"Paw prints, going up the garden!" cried Ravi in excitement, peering intently though the hole in the fence that Lance had been looking through. "Can't see Lucy though."

"Let me look," said Joel, pushing Ravi aside. Debbie looked next.

"I wonder where the paw prints go?" she asked, her voice rather muffled by the fence. "I can see a back gate – we might get a better look from there."

"We can do that!" said Lance, jumping up and down, partly in excitement, partly because he was cold. He waved his arm beyond the garden gate. "That's a lane that goes to a farm – they do 'pick your own strawberries' up there in the summer."

"But what about sledging?" asked Joel, looking rather longingly at the sledge.

"We can do that when we've found Lucy," said Debbie. "Come on everyone, let's get moving, it's cold standing still!"

"Good thing I'm getting used to walking with one arm," sighed Joel, as they shuffled and crunched their way through the snow, back to the side entrance of the park, quickly past Mrs Adamson's house and round the roads to the entrance to the lane, which was really little more than a farm track. Two tyre ruts of squashed snow wound their way like snakes up towards the farm Lance had mentioned, but for now the road was empty of vehicles. On one side of the lane the snow-laden hedgerows gave way to the back gates of the Salisbury Mews' gardens; on the other side a row of cottages with brightly coloured front doors stood out cheerfully against the white of the snow.

"Mrs Adamson's will be the last gate on this side," said Lance, indicating the hedgerows. "We should look for paw prints as we go, in case Lucy came this way."

"It's so pretty here, with the snow," admired Debbie, looking around. "God's creation is amazing!" As she spoke, she noticed a man wearing a navy uniform and carrying a briefcase, about to leave one of the cottages they had just passed. Her eyes grew round and her mouth dropped open.

"That's the same man as yesterday," she hissed, clutching Ravi's arm. "It's the handbag burglar!"

"Let's not jump to conclusions!" said Joel with a grin, turning round to look. Debbie smiled sheepishly and pulled herself together.

"OK, maybe he's not the burglar," she admitted, "but he was certainly in Mrs Adamson's road yesterday and he might have seen Lucy. I'm going to ask him." She broke into a shuffling run through the snow, closely followed by the others. "Excuse me," she called. The man ignored her, but appeared to change his mind about visiting the next cottage. Turning round, he walked swiftly back down the lane. Not to be put off, the little group caught up with him.

"Excuse me, we're looking for a cat," said Lance a little breathlessly. "A tortoiseshell one, quite big. I don't suppose you've seen her?"

"No," said the man brusquely, striding quickly away. Everyone shrugged as the man walked off.

"He was rude, but I don't think he's the burglar," said Debbie. "His badge said electricity something – he's obviously official."

"It could be fake," said Ravi. "He's hardly going to wear a badge saying 'Handbag Thief', is he? He might be knocking on doors, looking for old people to steal from. We could follow him – that might lead us to a clue."

"I don't think we should have anything to do with him," said Lance, firmly. "He's probably just a salesman. If he is a thief, the police can get him." Debbie tossed her head.

"Who cares about Mrs Adamson's stupid handbag, anyway? It's Lucy that matters."

They arrived at Mrs Adamson's back gate without having found any paw prints, which was disappointing. Lance was about to speak when he stopped in surprise and pointed to the ground. Although the gate was closed now, the snow had been trampled all around it.

"Zigzag footprints!" yelled Joel in amazement, staring at the ground. "Big ones, like the burglar's footprints round Ravi's shed! Surely that's a distinguishing mark?"

"Do you think Mrs Adamson's got a shed then?" asked Ravi, hardly able to believe his eyes.

"Probably, most people have," answered Lance. "We ought to go and look. A shed's just the sort of place a cat might get shut in by mistake."

Ravi's eyes shone with excitement. "And we have to see if the shed's been broken into! I can't believe these are the same footprints as the ones in my garden. This is a real mystery – we've got to solve it!" He turned the handle of the old wooden gate and gave it a push, but it wouldn't budge.

"Here, let me help," offered Lance. Ravi moved over and the two of them managed to push the solid wooden gate open with a loud creak.

"No paw prints," said Lance, peering into the snowy garden.

"But humans have been here!" said Joel. "Or at least one human. Look at all the zigzag footprints mashing up the snow! And there is a shed, round those bushes, see the corner sticking out?"

"We have to go and look," said Ravi.

"Into the dragon's lair?" stuttered Joel. "No way! You can, my friends. I choose life!"

Lance smiled. "I can't believe you sometimes, Joel, you're such a chicken!"

Joel looked mutinous. "Come on, Joel," wheedled Ravi. "The shed's so close!" Debbie frowned.

"For once in my life I agree with Joel. We should ask Mrs Adamson first."

"Ask Mrs Adamson?" cried Joel, waving his good arm for emphasis. "I'm not asking Mrs Adamson anything. I'm just not going into her garden, full stop!"

Ravi nodded. "If we go and tell her that her shed's been broken into, she'll probably blame us for that too."

"That's a good point," said Lance thoughtfully. "Maybe we should just look for Lucy, then sort out the shed problem when we get home."

"Good idea," agreed Debbie.

"I'll go with you to the shed, though, Rav," continued Lance, "in case Lucy's got shut in it. Just there and back, so we can let her out if we find her."

"OK," agreed Ravi. "It's not like it's criminal damage – I think this is my chance to be bold and courageous!"

"Bold and stupid more like!" cautioned Joel. "You might get turned into toads!"

Ravi grinned. "I'm willing to take that risk!"

"Hurry up then," said Debbie, shivering in the cold wind as she looked up at the leaden sky. "We *have* to get Lucy in the warm before it snows again or she might freeze to death."

"OK then Rav, ready?" asked Lance.

"We'll keep guard for you," offered Debbie. "But don't be long, it's cold just standing around."

"And if we see dragon's breath, we'll give you a shout!" promised Joel.

"Thanks," said Lance with a grin. "That would warm us up!"

Debbie and Joel watched Ravi and Lance until they disappeared from sight, then turned towards the road. A dark red van was trundling up the lane towards them, making a swishing noise as it swept the snow aside. "This is embarrassing," muttered Debbie. "Shall we close the gate?"

"Bit late," shrugged Joel, keeping close to the hedge to avoid being splattered by the slush as the van passed. But it didn't pass. Much to their consternation, the van drew up next to them and the driver's window opened. The driver was a young man, with a black woolly hat pulled down over his ears. Debbie's heart started to beat faster.

"Pretend to be looking for Lucy," hissed Joel, as the van's engine cut out.

"What do you think you're doing?" asked the driver suddenly and harshly. "Why's that gate open?"

"We're looking for a lost cat," replied Joel, trying to sound nonchalant.

"With a sledge?" snorted the man disbelievingly. "There have been some sheds broken into round here – I suppose I ought to call the police!" There was a brief, shocked silence.

"No, we're really looking for a cat," Debbie assured the man in the van.

"And the sledge isn't for carrying away the stolen goods?" snarled the man.

"No, we're going sledging when we've found her," retorted Debbie, staring boldly back. How dare he accuse them of stealing; the second person in two days! Joel was looking at the man too and what he saw made his mouth drop open. Round the edges of the man's hat, chunks of curly fair hair were sticking out! Realising that he was staring, Joel looked away and tried to think. Surely that was the same type of hair that Debbie had found in Ravi's shed? What about the man's footprints? He closed his eyes for inspiration and suddenly had an idea.

"I wonder if you'd come and look in this tree for me," he asked the man. "I'm not tall enough, but I think the cat might have gone up there and got stuck. See?" He pointed vaguely in the direction of an evergreen tree beyond the view of the man's window. The man craned his neck, but couldn't see where Joel was pointing, so with a sigh he climbed out of the van, took a few steps and stared up at the tree.

"I can't see a cat," complained the man. "You messing me about?"

Joel wasn't looking up at the tree, he was staring at the marks made in the snow by the man's boots. As he had guessed, they were large zigzag footprints.

EIGHT

More Surprises

With an effort, Joel looked away from the man's footprints, clear in the snow. "Sorry, I thought there might have been a cat in the tree, but it must have been a bird or something," he muttered, the colour draining from his face. He looked at Debbie, who was staring at the footprints. By the shocked look on her face, he knew what she was thinking. "I think we'll go sledging now, yeah?" he said, pushing Debbie away from the van. But as Debbie turned, she saw something else surprising. Someone was trying to stay hidden in the passenger seat of the van – and it was none other than the rude electricity man in the blue uniform!

"Come *on*, Debs," urged Joel, as she hesitated, but Debbie stood fixed to the spot, trying to hide her shock. Who were these men? Why were they together? Pretending not to have seen the second man, she blurted out the first thing she could think of.

"Would you look out for the cat for us?"

"Don't you think I've got better things to do with my time?" jeered the man with the black hat, climbing back up into his van and closing the door with a bang, which sounded harsh in the quietness of the snow.

"Um," said Debbie, swallowing hard. Her throat felt dry and her heart was thumping. "Yes, but if you were reading meters round here or anything like that, you could keep a look out."

"Well you've guessed it!" said the man, leering at her with piercing blue eyes. "Gas meters get old, they need changing. You want me to come and look at yours?"

"No thanks," said Debbie, stepping back. Suddenly she turned away. It didn't matter who these men were – as Lance had said, someone else could sort that out. "Let's go," she said loudly to Joel and they began to stride away down the lane together, sledge in tow.

As the man wound his window back up, he called, "You keep away from those sheds, OK?"

"Wow," said Joel, as the van burst into life and continued its way up the lane towards the farm. "Did you see the man's hair and footprints?"

"I did," nodded Debbie soberly. "Same as at Ravi's. And did you see the electricity man sitting in the passenger seat?"

"What, the man we talked to earlier?" asked Joel, sounding incredulous. "The one who was in Mrs Adamson's road yesterday? He was in the van?"

Debbie nodded. "Yes, him." Joel was still staring at Debbie in amazement when Ravi and Lance came bursting out of the gate and down the road towards them.

"Lucy wasn't there," Lance told them, slightly out of breath. "There were paw marks in the garden, but it was impossible to see where they went. The shed's *definitely* been burgled. It's just about empty and snow's been trampled all round, but no footsteps go down to the house. It looks like the stolen stuff was taken up to the back gate, like at Ravi's – that's another distinguishing mark!"

"We've done better than you, we've found the shed burglar," Debbie informed them, hardly able to believe her own words.

"You've *what*?" asked Ravi, looking round in surprise. "Where?"

"A man in a van going up the lane stopped and asked what we were doing," explained Joel. "I saw he had curly fair hair under his hat – like the hair Debs found in Ravi's shed! We should have got the registration number of the van, but I didn't think about it at the time."

"Me neither," admitted Debbie. "Joel got the man to get out and these footprints are his!" She walked back up the lane, pointed out the new set of footprints and explained everything. There was stunned silence when she had finished her tale.

"The man who stole my bike!" said Ravi eventually, shaking his head. "I can't believe I missed him!"

"And now he's done Mrs Adamson's shed too," added Joel. "And maybe loads of others, all over the town!"

Lance nodded gravely. "He could have done, though I still think . . ." he began, but Debbie interrupted him.

"I've just realised something else," she said in a

shocked voice. "The man that got out of the van, the one with the curly hair and zigzag footprints, he said they were checking *gas* meters, but the other man's badge said *electricity*."

"Are you sure?" asked Ravi. Debbie's voice sounded wobbly.

"Certain."

Joel nodded. "He did say that. Those men are fake for sure – and it looks like between them they could be the shed burglar *and* the handbag thief!"

Ravi looked a bit dazed. "How did we get into all this? Shed burglaries, missing cat, stolen handbag . . . this mystery's getting more mysterious all the time!"

"So what do we do now?" asked Joel.

"Look, I was going to say, I don't think we should get involved with the burglaries," said Lance firmly. "If those men are criminals – and it looks like they are – it's not safe for us to interfere. We'll find Lucy, then we'll go home and tell our parents about the shed and everything. They can decide what to do."

"I agree with that one hundred percent," agreed Debbie. "Sorry about the mystery and your bike, Rav, but Lucy . . ." She started trudging up the lane to hide the fact that tears had come to her eyes. The boys raised their eyebrows at each other and Joel groaned.

"Don't let's walk far. It's freezing out here and remember I've got a broken elbow!"

"Suppose we don't find Lucy?" Ravi asked in a quiet

voice so Debbie couldn't hear.

"We give up," replied Joel immediately, but Lance shook his head.

"I really think we'll find her. When we were praying I felt sure that we would – we need to trust in the Lord and at least do the very best we can."

Joel looked longingly at the sledge, then pulled it behind him with a sigh. "If we find Lucy quickly we've still got time to go sledging. Actually, what we need to do," he added loudly in a silly voice, grinning wickedly in Lance's direction, "is to get into the mind of the cat!" Lance couldn't help smiling.

"Joel, you're impossible sometimes!"

"Cream," carried on Joel, "Miaow, I'm thinking cream and mice, nice chewy mice . . ."

"Stop it, Joel," snapped Debbie, turning round, "that's sick!"

"Mice!" yelled Lance suddenly. "Joel might be right – there are barns a bit further up – maybe Lucy has gone up there to catch mice!" Putting on a spurt of energy, he started running up the lane as well as he was able in the snow. Round a corner, he stopped by a gate to a field and looked about at the collection of farm buildings that stood before him, some on one side of the road, some on the other. Most of them looked old and run down, apart from one newer-looking, ugly concrete building with a corrugated iron roof, which had a large padlock on the door. The buildings formed a bleak patch of darkness against the brilliant white around them.

"Ooh, the wind's even colder up here," complained Ravi with a shiver as he, Debbie and Joel joined Lance.

"That tarpaulin looks like it would rather be somewhere warmer too!" agreed Lance. A tatty black tarpaulin covering a pile of rubble flapped mournfully in the wind, as if trying to shed its load of snow and fly away.

"If I was that tarpaulin," observed Debbie, "I'd head for the south of France."

"Just our Operations Room would do," said Ravi with a grimace. "With the heating on. Let's look round quick, then we can do that!"

"Yes, let's," agreed Joel. "I wouldn't have thought this was a good place for cats, anyway; they like warmth. And the buildings are half falling down."

"The strawberries are good in summer though," said Lance. You have to go through this gate to get to the farmhouse and the . . ." Suddenly he stopped and gave a yell. "Cat's paw prints, under the gate!"

"She crossed the road," shouted Ravi excitedly, pointing in the direction of the paw prints.

"Lucy did come here!" yelled Debbie, breaking into a run.

"It might not be Lucy, it could be a farm cat," reasoned Joel as they followed the trail of paw prints to the back of the newer concrete building, where they stopped abruptly underneath the only window.

"Whatever cat it is, they're a good jumper," admired

Ravi, looking up. "That window's nearly higher than my head!"

"That's not a window, it's a hole," observed Joel. "No glass in it."

Debbie looked up. "Window or hole, we need to see into it!"

"I could give you a piggyback, Lance," suggested Ravi. "You should be able to see in then."

"OK, let's try it," agreed Lance. At the third attempt, he managed to hold on to Ravi's back and grab the slab of concrete that did for a window sill, to steady himself. "It's really dark in here," he called down, staring in through the hole. "I thought this place might be for farm machinery, but it's just full of junk. I can't see Lucy . . . hang on a minute, my eyes are getting used to the dark."

"Not too long, you're heavy," groaned Ravi. Suddenly Lance gave a yell and nearly fell off Ravi's back.

"Wow, you're not going to believe this!" He jumped down, his eyes shining with excitement. "I don't think it is junk in there – I think it's stuff from people's sheds!"

NINE

Stolen Goods

"Stuff from people's sheds?" repeated Joel incredulously. "Are you sure?" Lance was so amazed, he could hardly get the words out.

"Looks like it! There's bikes, garden chairs, tools, lawnmowers – even statues," he stuttered. He grinned round at his friends. "This must be where the shed thief's been hiding the stolen goods! Maybe your bike's in there, Rav!" They all looked round at each other in stunned amazement, then Joel groaned.

"Why are we always getting into trouble?"

"This isn't trouble, it's brilliant!" crowed Ravi, delighted by the discovery. "You wanted to help find my bike, remember? And now we have – well, probably!"

"And it's not us in trouble, it's the criminals who stole all that stuff," added Lance.

"Assuming it is stolen," said Joel.

"Either that or someone's got a weird collection going on," laughed Lance. "How many people do you know who collect lawnmowers?"

"Oh who cares about stupid lawnmowers?" wailed Debbie. "We're here to find Lucy, remember?"

"I couldn't see her," admitted Lance, "but if she can

jump that high she must be OK and it's sheltered in there, out of the snow and wind. If she is in there, she'll be fine till our parents or the police sort all this out. Now we'd better go – if someone finds us here, we could really be in trouble."

"But what if it's not Lucy?" asked Debbie. "We might need to keep looking for her. Couldn't we just call her, see if she comes?"

"I suppose we could check," replied Lance. "Just quickly."

This time it was Lance's turn to give Ravi a piggyback. "Lucy!" Ravi called into the hole. His voice sounded strange and a bit creepy as it echoed round the dark barn. At first there was no reply but the wind whipping round, rattling the tin roof. "I can't see my bike," Ravi informed his friends. "There are loads of bikes over by the door, but I can't see from here if any of them are mine, it's too dark."

"What about Lucy?" asked Joel, just as Ravi gave a yell.

"I heard a miaow!" he called down. "I hate to say this, but it didn't really sound like normal. It sounded sort of upset, like she might have hurt herself or something."

"I knew it!" gasped Debbie. "We've got to get in there!"

"Get real," scoffed Joel. "Did you see the padlock on the door?"

"One of us could get in through the window," retorted Debbie. "We've got to try!" Lance shook his head.

"That's not a good idea," he said, holding on to Ravi's

legs to stop him slipping off his back. "It could be dangerous." Joel was just about to voice his agreement when Ravi yelled back down again.

"I can see her, it is Lucy! Lucy, Lucy!" he called. "She's pacing up and down next to a stack of white plastic chairs, I can't see what's wrong. I think we're going to have to try and get in. I could look for my bike at the same time!"

Joel shook his head as Ravi jumped off Lance's back. "It would be better to go home. The sooner we get back and get help, the sooner Lucy can be rescued and we can get the police to look for your bike."

"We could run to our house," suggested Debbie. "Of all of our homes, ours is the nearest. Mum will be at home, she'll know what to do."

"OK, we'll do that," agreed Lance, picking up the sledge rope. "Let's go then!" But as he spoke, they heard the sound of an approaching engine.

"Maybe it's the farmer," said Ravi, turning towards the lane. "If he's got his keys with him we could ask him if he'd mind if we look for Lucy in the barn. We can pretend we don't know anything about the shed stuff, but I could have a sneaky look for my bike while we're in there!"

"I'm not sure . . .," began Lance.

"It's not the farmer!" yelled Joel suddenly. "It's the electricity van . . . or the gas van!"

"Hide!" yelled Ravi and they all stepped quickly back behind the concrete wall.

"Are you sure it's the same van?" Lance asked Debbie

and Joel, who both nodded.

"That's definitely it," confirmed Joel, peering round the corner. "As soon as it's gone by, we'll get out of here, yeah?" he said. But to the horror of the little group, the van didn't go by. It slowed down, then stopped in front of the building they were hiding behind, just a few metres away. They looked round at each other, stunned.

"Surely they're not checking the gas or electricity here?" whispered Joel. Lance shook his head.

"I don't think those men are anything to do with gas or electricity. If they were, there would be writing on the van, with the name of the company. I reckon they've come to look at their stolen stuff!"

"We'll find out," said Ravi grimly. They all held their breath as Ravi peered cautiously round the corner of the barn. "There's only one man in the van, the passenger seat's empty . . . He's a tall man, with a black woolly hat. Must be the man you saw in the lane – the man who stole my bike; I can't believe I'm looking at him! He's getting out of the van . . . he's carrying a big torch . . . he's got some keys out . . . " Ravi tapped the grey wall of the building they were hiding behind. "He's going to go in here!" Although they couldn't see what was happening, the others could hear the crunch of the man's boots in the snow, the rattle of keys and the creak as the door opened.

"He's gone in," Ravi informed them.

"Shall we run for it?" whispered Debbie.

"It might be better to wait till he's gone," suggested

Lance, swallowing hard. "I don't suppose he'll be long. We'll have to keep quiet though, or he might hear us."

"Ssh!" hissed Ravi urgently as the man reappeared. "He's wheeling a bike to his van! A green racing bike – looks like new! Maybe he's going to sell it. Does that make you sick or what?" They all heard the noise of the bike's wheels spinning as the man lifted it into the back of his van.

"What's he doing now?" asked Debbie after a pause. Ravi leaned right round the corner.

"He's in the back of the van," Ravi replied. "He's probably sorting out the space for another bike or something. Mine, maybe!" Suddenly he turned towards the others and said with determination, "Wait for me here, I'm going in," and before anyone could stop him he dashed round to the front of the building and ran in through the door.

"Rav!" Lance hissed desperately towards Ravi's swiftly departing back. As the man jumped out of the back of the van, Lance shot back behind the wall and stared at the others, dumbfounded.

"What did Rav do that for?" asked Joel. "He's mad!"

"Did the man see him?" asked Debbie, her eyes wide with fear. Lance shook his head.

"I don't think so." The three of them stood there for a minute, breathing hard, all sorts of thoughts going through their minds. Whatever was Ravi thinking of? Lance rubbed his gloved hands quietly together to get some warmth flowing. Now the cold he was feeling was more than the weather – a chill seemed to have settled in the pit of his stomach.

"What are we going to do now?" asked Debbie. "This is awful!"

"Ssh," warned Joel, as they heard the man whistling inside the barn. Something scraped on the floor, then after a while came the sound of another bike being wheeled to the van.

"I think we should . . ." began Lance, sounding worried, but his voice trailed off as he heard the clang of the barn door closing, then a loud click as the padlock snapped shut.

"Oh!" gasped Debbie. "Ravi's locked in!"

"At least the man didn't see him," said Lance with a grimace. "As soon as the van's gone we'll leg it, get someone to sort all this out – including Ravi." He peered round the wall to make sure the man was getting into his van, but his heart nearly stopped beating when he saw that the man wasn't going anywhere; he was standing still, torch in hand, staring down at the snow. "The man's seen our footprints!" he gasped in dismay. Lance's heart sank. Why hadn't he thought of that? He looked quickly round; where could they hide? But concealment was useless – wherever they went the man could just follow their trail in the snow! Lance closed his eyes and prayed a quick "Help!" as he heard the man's boots approach and crunch to a halt in front of them.

"Well now!" said the man, narrowing his eyes suspiciously at Debbie and Joel. "You're the kids hanging round the lane! And three of you now – decided to follow me, did you? Why was that?" Lance realised with a sinking heart that the man suspected that they knew about the contents of the building. He towered over them, making Lance feel small. Lance gulped. How were they going to get out of this?

TEN

The Rescue

"Well, speak up, what are you doing here?" growled the man. He glowered down at Lance, Debbie and Joel.

"We're still looking for our cat," replied Debbie in a small voice. The man narrowed his eyes at the little group.

"A cat? Really?" He sounded as if he didn't believe them.

"It's not exactly our cat," said Lance truthfully, attempting a polite smile. "It belongs to an old lady who lives in Salisbury Mews. We're looking for it for her."

"So why are you hiding here then?" asked the man suspiciously, crossing his arms.

"We followed her paw prints in the snow," answered Lance quickly, pointing to the ground under the window. Fortunately, although most had been well and truly trampled over, a few paw prints could still clearly be made out. "We think she must have gone in this window." The man visibly relaxed.

"Ah, I see," he nodded. Lance breathed an inner sigh of relief. It looked as if the man believed them now; the danger was over. "I'll go and have a look for you," the man continued, in a more even tone. "The last thing I want in there is a cat. What colour is it?" Lance turned pale. He had breathed too soon. If the man went back in the barn, he'd find Ravi!

"She's tortoiseshell, with a fluffy tail," answered Debbie, looking rather frightened. Recognition passed over the man's face and he leered savagely.

"So she's found a new home, has she? About time too. Always having kittens. If I find any, I'll drown them," he muttered, then his face creased into an unfriendly sneer. "Only joking!" Nobody smiled back.

"Perhaps we could look instead?" suggested Lance tentatively, trying to hide his trembling emotions. "We could save you the bother." They had to stop the man finding Ravi! The man turned on Lance fiercely.

"You are trespassing on my land! I'll look for your cat, you'll wait right there, then you'll get out of here and get out quick!" With that he strode away. He fiddled with the padlock, threw it down with a heavy thud into the snow and kicked the door open as if in a temper. Debbie looked too frightened to move.

"Oh no," groaned Joel. "Are we really trespassing?"

"I suppose we should have stayed on the path," admitted Lance, swallowing hard. "I can't believe all this has happened. We'd better pray right now, the Lord's our only hope."

"Good idea," agreed Debbie anxiously, closing her eyes. "Dear Lord, please help us, we've got ourselves in a mess and don't know what to do." Joel and Lance nodded agreement.

"And please, Lord," added Joel, "please stop the man finding Ravi."

"Yes," agreed Lance. "Please keep us all safe – including Lucy – and guide us so we know what to do next. Amen."

Just as his friends said a fervent, "Amen," to Lance's prayer, a cautious tapping sound coming from the other side of the wall made them jump.

"It's me," called Ravi in a hoarse whisper.

*   *   *

When Ravi had first run into the building, he had surprised even himself with his boldness. "I can't believe I'm doing this!" he thought, pausing briefly inside the door as he looked round for a good place to hide. He saw it straight away. The man's powerful torch stood on a wooden table, lighting up a large collection of bikes on the left wall of the barn, so Ravi ran to the opposite wall, where it was darkest. He scooted to a halt behind a higgledy-piggledy group of lawnmowers and grinned to himself. "Bold and courageous, that's what I am," he told himself proudly. He was just deciding whether to look for Lucy or his bike first when he heard the man's footsteps by the door.

Crouching down, Ravi watched the man stride purposefully to the row of bikes and examine each one in turn, whistling cheerfully. It seemed as if he was searching for something in particular. "Why should that man have those bikes?" Ravi thought in disgust, peering warily between lawnmower handles. "I bet none of them belong to him!" He felt like leaping up and telling the man how he felt, but knowing that that would be stupid he gritted his teeth, stayed hidden and looked round to get his bearings.

As Lance had said, the barn did look as if it held the contents of many sheds; it smelled a bit like a shed too, or maybe more like a garage – cold, damp, dusty and a bit oily. Many items had been grouped together. Apart from the row of bikes that the man was searching through and the assembled group of lawnmowers that Ravi was hiding behind, there was a collection of statues and birdbaths, various piles of garden tools and a large selection of tables and chairs; some in neat stacks, others just thrown on top of each other in untidy heaps. Smaller bikes were mixed up with children's ride-on toys – trains, cars, trikes, rockets; all shapes and sizes. And from where he crouched, Ravi could just make out the stack of white plastic chairs near where he had seen Lucy from the window.

"When the man goes out with the next bike, I'll find Lucy, get my bike, then get out before I'm seen," Ravi promised himself. It wasn't too long before the man had chosen the bike he wanted; a smart black mountain bike. Ravi watched him carefully as he separated it from the others and wheeled it out of the door. As soon as the coast was clear, Ravi sprang into action, picking his way quickly towards Lucy through the jumble of goods. But he hadn't quite reached the stack of chairs before the man returned, stamping the snow off his boots in the doorway.

Ravi dropped down quickly, right where he stood, his heart pounding so loudly that he was sure that the man would be able to hear it if he came any closer. But the man, with no idea that he was being watched, only came in as far as the torch. He picked it up from the table, turned it off with a loud click and turned back towards the door.

"He can't be going already!" thought Ravi anxiously. "I don't want to be locked in!" But the door was already closing and a split second later the padlock closed with a muffled snap. "That wasn't supposed to happen," Ravi muttered to himself, gulping in the sudden darkness. The wind moaned mournfully round the building and a cold draught blew under Ravi's collar. His heart sank. "Bold and courageous!" he reminded himself, feeling just about exactly the opposite, but a sudden miaow cheered him up. "Lucy!" he murmured, standing up again as his eyes grew accustomed to the dim light from the little window.

"Where are you, Lucy? It's OK, I won't leave you!" He measured up the window for size, in his mind. "I can't get my bike out of the window, but I can still save Lucy," he thought determinedly. He could pass her through the window to his friends and, if necessary, get out of it himself. Then they could go to the police and tell them about the bikes and all these other stolen goods.

"Lucy," he whispered. "Where are you?" Ravi made his way towards her, nearly tripping over a box of red-hatted garden gnomes on the way. And there she was, still pacing up and down next to the stack of plastic chairs!

"Lucy!" crooned Ravi affectionately, taking off his gloves and bending down to stroke her. "Are you OK? What are you doing here?" As Ravi leaned over, his eye caught on something which made him gasp. Three tiny tortoiseshell kittens were curled up on top of the stack of chairs, fast asleep on a purple blanket that had been dumped there. "Kittens!" gasped Ravi aloud, hardly able to believe his eyes. "Lucy, you've got kittens!" Lucy mewed loudly at his feet. He picked her up to give her a cuddle, but she struggled and jumped down, then tried to reach something with her paw. With a beating heart, Ravi realised what it was – a little ginger kitten had fallen off the blanket nest and was stuck in a gap behind the chair legs. Lucy couldn't reach it and the kitten was too small to be able to move. "Oh, little Kitty!" gasped Ravi, reaching out his hand to pick it up. Its little eyes were still closed but it mewed silently. "Oh, little Kitty," he said again. It looked more like a tiny scrap of fur than a kitten, with a tail and paws so small they barely existed. As Ravi placed it carefully down with the other kittens, Lucy jumped up, curled herself round them all and began to wash the little stray ginger one. Ravi stroked Lucy, too full of emotion to speak, but Lucy began to purr loudly.

Ravi had been so engrossed in what he was doing that he had only vaguely heard the sound of voices outside. Then there was a sudden bang which startled him. The door was kicked open with a slam and the same man who had taken the bikes stood framed in the light of the doorway, sweeping his torch around the building. Ravi melted into the shadows behind the chairs, breathing hard, trying not to panic. Something must be wrong. The man seemed angry; why?

Ravi closed his eyes and swallowed hard, resisting the temptation to run, desperately hoping that the torch wouldn't pick him out. After a few seconds, the man, muttering obscenities, began what appeared to be a search for something, starting near the door, moving things about and kicking tools and other items out of his way. Ravi thought quickly. What was the man looking for – maybe something to go with the bikes – panniers, perhaps? But why should he be in a temper about that? The voices he had vaguely heard outside . . . maybe he had been talking to Lance, Debbie and Joel? Perhaps they had told him that he was in the barn? Ravi was worried. He had to check! Ravi crept quietly towards the window, keeping to the shadows as much as possible. Checking that the man was still occupied elsewhere, he tapped on the wall and called out to his friends.

"Rav, is that you?" he heard Lance call back.

"Yes!" replied Ravi quietly. "Does the man know I'm in here?"

"No!"

"Good!" whispered Ravi, almost bursting with relief and his surprise. "Guess what? Lucy's got kittens!"

"Kittens?" exclaimed Debbie, from the other side of the

wall, then she gasped in fear. "Don't let the man see them!"

"Rav, hide!" hissed Lance. He had hardly finished speaking when they heard the man's voice echoing round the large barn, clear and triumphant.

"Ha! Got you!"

"Oh no," mouthed Debbie, covering her face with her hands. "He'll drown Lucy's kittens! And what will he do to Ravi? We've got to stop him!"

"There's nothing we can do now," swallowed Lance. "We prayed. Now we'll have to hope for a miracle." With beating hearts, Debbie, Joel and Lance waited for the man's return. He re-appeared, not with Ravi, but carrying a much thinner-looking Lucy by the scruff of her neck.

"Right, got your cat, now get out of here!" the man ordered them, handing Lucy rather roughly to Debbie, who stepped forward to take her.

"Thanks," said Lance. So the man hadn't seen Ravi. Or he wasn't saying that he had. And what about the kittens, had he seen them? He and Joel looked at each other. What should they do now?

"Well off you go then," said the man impatiently, crossing his arms.

"Of course, thanks for the cat," said Lance. He set off slowly towards the lane, pulling the sledge behind him, desperately trying to decide what to do. How could they leave the kittens? How could they leave Ravi? But what else could they do? He could feel the man's eyes watching them as they walked away.

ELEVEN
Precious Cargo

It was difficult walking away from the barn, knowing that they were leaving Ravi and the kittens behind. "We'll go round the corner, then stop," Lance told the others quietly. "When the van's gone we'll go back."

"That might be too late! The man might be taking the kittens right now," wailed Debbie, struggling to keep hold of Lucy, who was mewing pitifully and trying to get away. "Poor Lucy, she's so thin! And she wants to get back to her babies. This is awful!"

"There's Rav too," agreed Lance grimly.

"He's so stupid!" said Joel crossly. "I can't believe he just ran in . . . and Lucy's stupid too! Why did she have to come here to have kittens, when she's got a perfectly good home to have them in? Mrs Adamson's can't be that awful – for a cat!"

"She's just an animal, she doesn't understand," replied Debbie, sounding close to tears.

"The van's coming this way!" warned Lance suddenly, hearing the approaching engine. They all marched forward and Lance waved cheerfully as the van passed them. Joel raised his eyebrows.

"Your new best friend?" Lance grimaced back.

"Better he thinks we're friendly than that we're on to him. If it hadn't been for Lucy's paw prints under the window hole, we'd have been well in trouble. Right, the van's gone! Quick, Debs, you run to Mrs Adamson's with Lucy. Joel and I will go and rescue Rav and the kittens."

"But what if the man's got the kittens in his van?" cried Debbie, still struggling to keep hold of Lucy.

"We'll just have to hope not," replied Lance grimly.

"Help!" said Debbie in desperation. "Lucy wants to get down, I can't hold her . . ." With a twist and a leap Lucy jumped away and ran back up towards the farm. "Oh no," cried Debbie in despair. "Now everything's going wrong!"

"Come on, Debs, we'll save them all," Joel encouraged his sister, slapping her on the back with his gloved hand. "We ought to stay together anyway."

"That's true," admitted Lance, turning back towards the farm. "Staying together would be sensible. OK, come on then, let's all follow Lucy! Remember, we did pray and nothing is impossible with God!"

Hurriedly retracing their steps, the three soon arrived back at the group of farm buildings. Ravi surprised them by leaning out of the hole in the wall of the concrete building and waving. "Hey, am I pleased to see you!" he called as they approached at a stumbling run. "I hoped you'd be back soon – Lucy beat you though, she jumped in ages ago! Anyway, here's the plan – I'll pass you the kittens out one by one, then the blanket they're on. You can put the blanket on the sledge and we can take the kittens home on that!"

"Thank goodness you're all right!" called Debbie. "So the man didn't see you?" Ravi grinned cheerfully.

"No, I stayed hidden!"

"You don't deserve to be rescued!" called back Joel.

"Of course I do!" laughed Ravi. "I'm the hero, bold and courageous, I've got it all sorted! Anyway, I don't need rescuing, I can get out easily now – I've made a stack of things to climb on! Ready? I'll get the first kitten. Quickly now – can't let them get cold!" Joel rolled his eyes in mock desperation, but couldn't help smiling.

"Well done, Rav," said Lance, relief in his voice. "I was wondering how we'd ever get you out of there!"

"I'm so glad the kittens are still here," sighed Debbie, as Ravi passed them out to Lance's up-stretched arms one by one, first a tiny ginger one, followed by three little tortoiseshell ones, then Lucy jumped out too. Lance placed the kittens gently into Debbie's upturned hat, which made an excellent nest.

"Oh, they are so tiny!" crooned Debbie as she cradled her precious cargo. "Their eyes are still closed! Are you sure it's OK to move them? What if they die on the way home?"

"Don't panic, Debs," said Joel, peering at the kittens in her hat as Ravi threw the purple blanket out of the window, which Lance quickly picked up and shook out. "It's got to be better than leaving them here."

"We'll just have to do the best we can," agreed Lance,

trying not to panic himself. "But we can't put the kittens on top of this," he groaned, frowning at the blanket. "They'll get cold or roll off."

"Think pitta bread," suggested Joel, "with kittens as the filling!"

"Great idea!" replied Lance. Quickly folding the blanket, he laid it on the sledge and formed a neat pocket into which Debbie gently laid her hat with the kittens snuggled up inside. Lucy jumped straight in to join them. Debbie gently folded the edge over so that none of them could fall out, leaving a small hole for air.

"They should stay warm inside that," she decided with a sigh of relief. "I'm glad Lucy's in there, she'll keep them safe. And carrying her was impossible. The Lord knew we'd need the sledge today!"

"Stop fussing, Debs, we need to get out of here!" Joel urged her as Ravi threw something black out of the window, then jumped out himself, landing in the soft snow with a thud.

"Mission accomplished!" he announced with a grin, brushing the snow off his clothes, then picking up the black object. "And what do you think of this?"

"Is it Mrs Adamson's?" asked Debbie in amazement, staring at the black leather handbag that Ravi was triumphantly holding up. "It's got a gold clasp!"

"Not bad, eh?" smiled Ravi, full of his achievement. "I found it on the floor in there."

"You can't take that!" countered Lance, horrified.

"That's handling stolen goods!"

Joel snorted. "And what if it's not Mrs Adamson's? There must be thousands of lost black handbags in the country! I can't believe you sometimes, Rav, you're such an idiot!" Ravi looked crestfallen.

"Do you think I should I throw it back?" he asked.

"Now you've put your fingerprints all over it?" gasped Joel. "Good idea!"

"I'm wearing gloves," said Ravi.

"Oh please!" yelled Joel.

"Can't we just stop arguing and go?" begged Debbie.

"Now you've got it you'd better just bring it," said Lance impatiently, picking up the rope of the sledge and pulling it gently. "Come on, let's move!" The sledge swished slowly away through the soft snow and Debbie walked anxiously alongside, watching the blanket for any signs of trouble.

"Do we have to go to Mrs Adamson's?" asked Joel as they hurried back down the lane as fast as they safely could with their kitten cargo.

"Yes," replied Lance firmly. "It's her cat. Anyway, she's nearer than any of our homes." Ravi nodded.

"And I've hopefully got her handbag. Will you carry it for me, Debs?"

"No way! Carry it yourself!"

"But I can't carry a handbag!" retorted Ravi, holding it out at arm's length.

"And you think I want to carry a black granny

handbag?" snorted Debbie. "Especially a stolen one?"

"Put it on the sledge then, for goodness sake!" said Lance, exasperated. "And phone Tina, Rav, yeah, do something useful, see if she can meet us at Mrs Adamson's?"

"Good idea, or we might get eaten alive," agreed Joel. "We can go in the back gate, it'll be quicker." Lance shook his head.

"Better not, we'd frighten Mrs Adamson to death, appearing at the back door. She'd probably think we'd come to steal something else! We'll go round to the front, it won't take that much longer."

"She'll be surprised to see the kittens," said Debbie.

"And to see how much thinner Lucy is," agreed Joel.

"I don't understand why the man didn't give the kittens to you, with Lucy," said Ravi, holding his phone to his ear. "He definitely saw them; I could see him from where I was hiding. He stopped and stared at them."

"Didn't you hear what he said to us?" asked Lance. "He said if he found any kittens he'd drown them!"

Ravi's cheerful expression changed to one of horror. "I didn't hear him say that. That is so sick . . ." He shook his head in disbelief. "Nicking bikes is bad enough, but drowning innocent kittens . . . I hope he goes to prison!"

"There are some really evil people in this world," agreed Lance. "Isn't Tina answering?" Ravi shook his head.

"No, shall I give up?"

"No, try again, she might be driving."

"By the way, did you find your bike in the barn, Rav?" asked Joel, as they turned out of the lane.

"Or Gita's trike?" added Debbie.

"My bike wasn't there," admitted Ravi, still holding his phone to his ear. "I hope it hasn't already been sold. I didn't have time to look for the trike; I was too busy finding things to stand on, so I could get out of the window. I knew the kittens would die if we didn't get them to Lucy quickly. They'd have got cold, or starved. I thought, if you weren't back soon I'd have to work out how to get the kittens out on my own. I was praying you'd come back! You don't know how great it was to see you!"

As they left the lane and turned on to the road, Joel suddenly let out a yell. "It's the van again!" They all turned to look. Sure enough, the red van was making its way towards the lane that they had just left. Both men were in it now; the man in the suit and the man with the black hat. The van paused at the junction, its indicator light reflecting orange, on and off, on the snowy road.

"The men were staring at us!" yelled Ravi, as the van turned into the lane and set off up towards the farm.

"We'd better hurry!" cried Joel. "They'll have noticed there's four of us now!" Ravi grimaced.

"And they'll see the stack of stuff I made by the window and know we've been in there!"

"And that we've taken the kittens," added Debbie.

"And they can follow our sledge trail!" yelled Lance,

suddenly picking up speed. "Wherever we go they can find us!"

"Tina!" yelled Ravi suddenly into his phone. "Tina, at last, help! Can you come to Mrs Adamson's quick? It's an emergency!"

TWELVE

The Return

There was a tense silence as Ravi listened to Tina's reply and the sledge continued to swish through the snow.

"Well we've found Lucy . . . yes, and she's had kittens! . . . and there's a man after us, possibly two – well there might be – look, I haven't got time to explain it all now, but please hurry! . . . OK, see you in a few minutes then." Ravi let out a deep breath and closed his phone.

"So she's coming?" asked Lance anxiously.

"As soon as she can," replied Ravi, sounding relieved. "I can't wait to give Mrs Adamson her handbag!"

"Huh!" said Joel as they turned the corner into Salisbury Mews. "She'll just as likely think you stole it and now you feel guilty, so you've brought it back!" Suddenly he gave a yell. "Oh, Lance, look out, the sledge is going to tip over!" As Lance had turned the corner, the sledge had veered dangerously to the side. Joel reached out to steady it, but his hand reached the back of the sledge just too late. They all watched in horror as the sledge flipped up and over, as if in slow motion. Lucy jumped out just as the sledge landed face downwards in the snow with a dull thud.

"The kittens!" screamed Debbie.

"Take the other end, Rav!" cried Lance urgently, grabbing the front of the sledge. Ravi took hold of the back and the two of them lifted it carefully with beating hearts.

"Are the kittens OK?" asked Joel, hovering anxiously over Debbie, who was kneeling in the snow, feeling in the folds of the blanket for her hat. Lance and Ravi placed the sledge carefully back down on to the pavement.

"Sorry everyone," said Lance, with a beating heart. "I was going too fast. I didn't realise the sledge was tipping."

"It's OK, the kittens seem all right," replied Debbie weakly, checking the kittens and stroking Lucy, who was pacing up and down next to her, nosing into the blanket and mewing. "But this is starting to feel like a nightmare. Can we go quick? I just want to get this over with now!"

"Look, we're nearly at Mrs Adamson's, Debs," encouraged Joel, noticing that his sister was brushing tears from her eyes. "Why don't you just carry the kittens in your hat the last bit of the way?"

"I think I will," Debbie replied, gingerly getting up from the snow with her precious bundle. Ravi noticed that she was shivering.

"Do you want to borrow my hat?" he offered. Debbie shook her head.

"No, it's OK, thanks anyway, I'm not really that cold," she said, trying to be brave, although she didn't feel it. "I'm partly shaking 'cause it's so scary. I'll be all right in a minute, once the kittens are safe. And Lucy. And us!"

She looked down the length of the road. Mrs Adamson's house seemed like miles away. Surely Salisbury Mews hadn't been that long yesterday? Ravi patted her arm.

"You're doing great!"

Lance grimaced. He did hope they would all be all right in a minute. But what would they do if the men came back to find them? Keeping his eyes and ears open for any sign that the van might be approaching, he picked up the blanket and bundled it quickly back on to the sledge. "Dear Lord Jesus, we need your help," he prayed. Ravi picked up the handbag and Lucy ran round Debbie's feet, mewing.

"Lucy, get out from my feet!" begged Debbie anxiously. "Can someone please run and ring on Mrs Adamson's doorbell?"

"I will!" volunteered Ravi, breaking into a run. It didn't take him long to reach Mrs Adamson's gate. He took the path in long strides and rang on the door bell urgently, twice. By the time Mrs Adamson answered the door, Ravi was jumping impatiently from one foot to the other.

"You!" said Mrs Adamson in grim recognition as she saw Ravi standing there. "What is the meaning of this? And what is so desperately important that you have to ring the bell *twice*?" Her face hardened even further when she saw what he was carrying. "That is my handbag!" she said fiercely, snatching it out of Ravi's outstretched hand. At that moment she noticed the other boys approaching. Lance was pulling the sledge with the purple blanket trailing along behind and Joel was shuffling along as quickly as he could with one arm in the sling. "What on earth is going on here?" she snapped.

"Can we come in and tell you?" asked Lance as he reached the doorstep, looking round anxiously to see if they were being followed. "Please?"

"Absolutely not! Get away, all of you, or I shall phone the police!"

"But there might be men after us!" said Joel, joining the growing group.

"Rubbish!" said Mrs Adamson, then she noticed Debbie at the gate, cradling her hat in her hands. "Whatever . . .?" began Mrs Adamson, then she saw Lucy, rubbing round Debbie's legs.

"My Lucy!" cried the old woman. "Oh my little Lucy, come here, darling!"

"We found her," said Lance.

"And your handbag," added Ravi.

"And your shed's been burgled," Joel informed her. Mrs Adamson's eyes grew round with surprise as she looked at the group's earnest, anxious faces.

"And here are Lucy's kittens!" said Debbie with a tearful smile, reaching the group on the doorstep. "Please, we need to get them into the warm."

Lucy, who had been hanging round Debbie's feet, ran in the house as the old lady asked in surprise, "Just a minute, did you say, 'kittens'?"

Then Ravi saw a sight that filled him with relief. Tina's

little yellow car was making its way up the road towards them. "It's Tina!" he yelled, waving frantically. "Tina, we're over here!" Tina waved in return as she pulled up slowly and parked by the kerb.

"Are you all OK?" she asked, slamming the car door and running up the path. "Where's the man who's trying to get you?"

Ravi pointed vaguely in the direction of the farm. "Sort of, up there."

"Mrs Adamson," said Tina firmly, looking first at the worried faces of the young people, then at Mrs Adamson's startled expression. "May we come in?"

THIRTEEN

Bonfire and Marshmallows

"It's brilliant of your mum and dad to let us have a bonfire," said Lance to Debbie and Joel as the four friends sat on a log later that evening, toasting marshmallows over the last glowing embers of the fire.

"Especially after our shed trap caught your dad," agreed Ravi.

"They're pretty good parents, really," admitted Joel, passing the marshmallow bag along the log.

Debbie nodded. "Anyway, Dad's enjoyed the bonfire as much as we have. I thought he was never going to leave us in peace! Mm, the smell of smoke – I love it!"

"I know what you mean," said Ravi, poking the embers with a stick. "You just have to keep watching real fire. It's the way the flames are continually changing and shimmering."

"Hey, listen to the poet," grinned Joel. Ravi gave him a friendly shove on his good arm, which made the log wobble and they all nearly fell off.

"Watch it!" warned Debbie, struggling to hold her balance. "If we fall off the log we'll get wet and cold. And I like the warmth," she added, holding her hands up to the fire.

"I'm glad Lucy's in the warm now," sighed Lance. "And those little kittens. Weren't they just so cute?"

"Oh, hey," remembered Ravi, "I never told you why Lucy was miaowing in the barn – remember that? The ginger kitten had fallen off the blanket in between some chairs and Lucy couldn't get to it. But I rescued it!"

"Well done, Rav – you really are the hero, bold and courageous," teased Joel, clapping him on the back, then he looked up in surprise. "Oh, here's Tina! Hi Tina!"

"Hello!" called Tina cheerfully, closing the back door and walking over to join the others by the fire. "I'm glad I've got my coat on – I didn't expect to find you outside! Is there room for me?"

"'Course," said Debbie. "It's great to have you!"

"Come join the party," agreed Joel, as they shuffled along the log to make room. Debbie gave Tina a stick and the bag of marshmallows.

"Oh, thanks very much!" said Tina, spearing a marshmallow. "How wonderful! But I didn't come round to eat your food, although that's very nice! I've come to talk to you."

"That sounds scary!" said Lance.

"Some of it's good," Tina corrected him with a smile. "But I'll get the serious stuff out of the way first. I know you said you prayed together about getting Ravi's bike back and finding Lucy. You did find Lucy, plus kittens, which is fantastic, but I'd like to remind you about not speaking to strangers."

"They spoke to us first!" retorted Debbie.

"Not always, Debs," Joel reminded her. "We went up to the man in the suit and asked if he'd seen Lucy."

"And you got the man in the hat to get out of the van, Joel!" remembered Debbie.

"That's not good," said Tina seriously. "Promise me you'll never do that again! Also, none of you should have gone off the path and frankly, Ravi, I'm surprised at you going into that barn." Ravi grinned at her, but Tina looked sternly back.

"It's not funny, Rav, it could have had serious consequences."

"But I was being bold and courageous, like Joshua at the battle of Jericho," argued Ravi. "I read about it yesterday in my Bible notes." There was a short silence while Tina pondered this over.

"The trouble is, Ravi, you used the verse out of context," she replied. "God told Joshua exactly what to do; march round Jericho, blow trumpets – you know the story. *Then* he told Joshua to be bold and courageous doing *that*. My guess is that you went in the barn just because you wanted to." There was another pause, while the fire crackled and spat.

"You're right," admitted Ravi. "I wanted to get my bike back and I didn't see why that thief should have it."

"I appreciate your honesty," said Tina with a nod. "Well, the Lord answered your friends' prayers and graciously kept you safe and you did a great job, rescuing the kittens! But running into the barn, Ravi, really was a bad idea." Ravi thought for a minute, his face glowing in the warmth of the bonfire.

"Ah, but if I hadn't gone in, I wouldn't have been able to save the kittens!"

"You could have phoned me," said Tina. "We could have got Animal Rescue to come out, or something like that."

"We should have done that," agreed Lance.

"I can't believe we didn't think of that ourselves," nodded Debbie. "That would have been much less scary!"

"Does that mean I'm not the hero?" asked Ravi mournfully.

Tina smiled. "In a way you're all heroes, but I want you all to promise me that you'll not take risks like that again. Not ever!" Ravi looked down at his feet.

"I guess I let my anger take over," he admitted with a sigh.

"So you promise?"

"I promise," agreed Ravi.

"And the rest of you?" persisted Tina, looking round at their serious faces. "All of you?"

"We promise," they agreed.

"Great," said Tina with a sigh. "Praying is good, but you can't just assume you'll get everything you ask for. Do your parents give you everything you want?"

"No!" came four definite voices in unison.

"Why not?" asked Tina.

"'Cause they're mean!" replied Joel with a grin.

"They're not mean!" protested Debbie. "I suppose if we ask for something that's like, selfish, or greedy or something, they say no."

"Or dangerous," added Lance.

"Well that's it," said Tina. "Our heavenly Father knows what's best for us and doesn't give in to us behaving like spoilt children."

Debbie grimaced. "I hate spoilt children!"

Lance nodded thoughtfully. "So we need to pray, then listen for the answer before we assume we've got what we want. I think I get that now. I sort of did before, but now I really get it."

"And God's the boss, not the servant," added Joel. "Like, he tells us what to do, not the other way round!"

"That's it exactly!" Tina congratulated them. "Prayer is to bring us closer to God, to get to know what he wants and likes and enjoy his company as his children. He's not just a vending machine – push the right buttons and goodies come out!"

"That conjures up a weird image," said Ravi, lifting his eyebrows.

"That's what God's *not* like, Ravi," groaned Tina. "Anyway, enough of the sermon – now on to the good news!"

FOURTEEN

Tina's Surprise

"Good news," repeated Joel, brightening up. "I like the sound of that!"

"Three bits of good news!" said Tina cheerfully. "Firstly, you'll be glad to know, the police caught those two men red-handed in the barn and took them in for questioning."

"That's great!" yelled Ravi and the others whooped agreement. When the noise had died down, Tina continued.

"Secondly, Mrs Adamson had pet insurance for Lucy. They offer a reward for the safe return of a missing animal." The group looked at each other in astonishment.

"A reward?" asked Ravi.

"Money? And Mrs Adamson's giving it to us?" gasped Debbie. Tina smiled and nodded.

"How much?" asked Joel.

"Enough for a bike?" added Lance quickly. "If Ravi doesn't get his bike back, the money could be useful." Tina thought for a moment.

"You could probably get a nice second-hand one."

"But I don't think it would be fair for me to take all the money," objected Ravi. "After all, we did this together."

"Not the hero now, then, Rav?" asked Joel with a grin. Ravi grinned sheepishly back.

"I did find the handbag!"

"Yes, that's very true," said Tina with a smile. "By the way, after you left I had a serious talk with Mrs Adamson about not trusting people who appear to be official. So you think you'll use the reward money to buy a bike for Ravi then? Maybe this is the way the Lord is answering your prayer – instead of getting Ravi's old bike back, the Lord is providing a different one!"

"That's amazing really," said Debbie. "I don't think we can argue with that."

"Me neither," said Lance and Joel nodded agreement. Ravi looked round at his friends, rather overcome by their generosity.

"Well if you're sure, how about you all come to the bike shop and help me choose?"

"And if there's any money over, we could get more marshmallows!" said Joel, flapping the empty bag mournfully. "Or extra Easter eggs!"

"Or a little trike for Gita," suggested Debbie, "if she doesn't get hers back."

"Just a minute," Tina warned them. "There's a little, sort of, snag. Mrs Adamson wants to give you the money herself. She's invited you to tea tomorrow."

"Oh that's nasty!" groaned Joel. "I hope you said no. Even marshmallows aren't worth that pain! Anyway, we said we'd go sledging in the snow tomorrow as we didn't get to go today."

"I can't believe you sometimes, Joel, you're so mean," Debbie said, glaring at her brother along the log.

"Actually, I said I thought you would go," replied Tina. "I was counting on your better feelings!"

"We'll go if we're allowed," agreed Lance. "Won't we? We could always go sledging in the morning." He looked round at his friends, who nodded, albeit a little glumly. Tina grinned.

"Excellent! So, on to the third and last bit of good news . . . at least, I hope you'll think it's good news. Mrs Adamson has decided to keep all the kittens, but let the four of you name one each and go and visit it whenever you like!"

"So it's sort of like, we get a kitten, but it lives at Mrs Adamson's?" asked Debbie, struggling to take the information in. Tina nodded.

"Exactly. And you don't even have to buy food for it – just toys and treats!"

"I get a kitten!" yelled Lance, shooting up off the log. "Oops, sorry!" he apologised as the log rolled and everyone nearly fell off. "But I've always wanted a cat of my own and now this is my chance! Tomorrow I'm going to the pet shop and I'm going to buy loads of kitten toys!"

"Don't get too excited!" warned Joel. "It'll live at Mrs Adamson's, remember?"

"Surely that can't be too awful," countered Tina.

"If you think about it, she wasn't that bad even when

we were there the first time," reasoned Debbie. "She even laughed once!"

"Really?" asked Tina. "I don't think she laughs very often. You must have really cheered her up!"

"Well, she cackled," said Joel, imitating an evil chuckle. The boys laughed and even Tina grinned, but Debbie frowned.

"She did not laugh like that! It was when she laughed I realised she was actually pleased we were there."

"Me too," said Ravi. "And if you look at it from her point of view, it must have looked suspicious that after we left she noticed that her handbag had gone."

Tina nodded agreement. "She made a mistake, but nobody's perfect and even the worst people can change. Remember we talked about Zacchaeus the other day and how nobody wanted to visit him, but all he needed was a chance, which Jesus gave him?"

"We've been talking about that," said Debbie.

"That's great!" said Tina. "So would you be willing to give Mrs Adamson that chance? You must admit, she was quite a different person once she realised that you went to look for Lucy. I don't think she expected anybody to care."

"I was really surprised how nice she was to us, when she realised that we're not horrible yobs," admitted Joel.

"And she was really grateful that we saved Lucy and the kittens and kept saying thank you," added Debbie.

"I suppose everyone deserves a chance," nodded Lance. "And I love the idea of having my own kitten!"

"Me too!" agreed Ravi. "But can I ask you all a really big favour? Would any of you mind if I have the ginger one? That's the one that had fallen off the nest Lucy had made, the one I rescued. *Please*?"

"'Course," said Debbie. "Anyway, I want the kitten that looks most like Lucy!"

"No problem," agreed Lance.

Joel grinned wickedly. "So what are you going to call yours, Rav – 'Hero'?" They all laughed.

"You know what, I just might!" yelled Ravi, getting up and punching the air in delight. "And I bet he'll be bold and courageous! 'Hero' – I can't wait to meet him!"

Also available from Dernier Publishing:

The Treasure Hunt
by J. M. Evans

Ravi, Debbie, Joel and Lance's first exciting mystery adventure. Who is in the back of the white lorry and why are they there? Prayer, faith and their Bible knowledge all help, but when the case takes an unexpected turn, the friends also need to be courageous and obedient. Will they find out what is going on and find the real treasure? For ages 8-11.

"The best book I've ever read!" — *Emily*

ISBN 978 0 9536963 1 4

London's Gone
by J. M. Evans

London has been bombed by terrorists. Maria watched in horror as the smoke rose from the direction of London. Now she must make a hazardous journey to safety with her sister and a Christian friend, but is anywhere safe now? For Maria, the journey is also inside herself as she begins to discover a side to life that she did not know existed. A thrilling drama full of suspense. For ages 12+

"I just couldn't put this book down!" — *Jilly*

ISBN 978 0 9536963 2 1

**Beech Bank Girls – Every girl has a story
by Eleanor Watkins**

Six teenage friends draw nearer to God and each other
through real life issues in a moving, honest and fun way.
Amber, Holly, Willow, Annie, Rachel and Chloe share
their laughter, their tears, their hopes, their fears and their
secrets with each other and with us. Miracle and party
included! Chick lit for ages 10-14.

ISBN 978 0 9536963 4 5

Find all these and more at www.dernierpublishing.com
*Also available from your local book shop and on-line book
store.*